Annemarie Nikolaus: Broken Rules

"**Broken Rules**". 2nd revised edition, 2020
1° edition's title: "Past Crimes"
Translated by Lisa Rosenblatt
Originally published in German as: "Verjährt"
Written by Annemarie Nikolaus
Copyright © 2013-2020 Annemarie Nikolaus, F-03240 Tronget/Allier
All rights reserved
Cover © 2020 Design: Annemarie Nikolaus, Foto: 2018 Neil Williamson – modified -.
https://www.flickr.com/photos/neillwphoto/44660132401
CreativeCommons Attribution-ShareAlike 2.0 Generic (CC BY-SA 2.0)
ISBN 9782902412686

ANNEMARIE NIKOLAUS

BROKEN RULES

HISTORICAL SHORT STORIES

Contents

The Twelfth Night

Treganna, Cornwall, Christmas Eve 1072

A powerful storm roared around the Great Hall of Treganna, drowning out again and again the noise of the castle's celebrating servants. Then some of them choked on their laughter; others made the sign of the cross and looked around in fright. The dogs, which on other days were scuffling for bones, lay peacefully under the tables, attracting attention only with an occasional whimper.

The fires in the two huge fireplaces had trouble asserting themselves against the constant pressure of the wind. Smoke drifted all the way to the High Table where Sir Geoffrey, the new Lord of Treganna Castle, sat with his family.

Young Amis, his son, coughed as he inhaled the smoke. As he struggled harder and harder for air, Caitlin patted him on the back and then offered him a mug of water.

Concern was in her eyes, and she smiled compassionately. "Drink; you'll feel better then." With all hope he would choke on it. How she hated him, her stepbrother, even more than the Norman who had forced her mother into marriage. May god prevent Treganna from falling into the hands of this weakling one day; after all, she was the true heir.

A shudder ran over Amis as the storm suddenly whistled in a higher pitch.

"Are you freezing?" Sir Geoffrey wrapped him tighter in his warm plaid.

"No, Father. I was simply frightened."

"By this little bit of wind?" Sir Geoffrey sounded a little annoyed after all. "So close to the sea, it has more power than you're used to from... back home."

"Nay, My Lord." Caitlin again put on a worried mien. "That's not the storm singing out there... These are..." She let her voice fade away.

Amis paled and stared at her, his eyes wide open.

"Caitlin! You are not to feed such superstition."

"How dare you say such a thing, My Lord! What do you know of our land?" Outraged Caitlin leapt up, not letting even her mother's irate shout hold her back.

Not long after that, Amis came into Caitlin's bedroom. "Sister, what is it that you are forbidden to tell me of?"

Caitlin rolled her eyes at the loathed address. "What it is? Your father does not want me to tell you what you can't learn from him." She waved him closer to the fire and lowered her voice. "Wind, yes, you could call it that. But it doesn't come from the sea. It's the Wild Hunt seeking revenge during the nights until Epiphany."

The boy cleared his throat and and tried to give his voice a deeper, more mature sound. "Caitlin, now really, that's just superstition."

She pulled him next to her onto the windowsill and whispered: "Have you not seen the fear in the servants' faces?" Caitlin suppressed a triumphant smile as the boy's gaze began to waver with uncertainty. "But you mustn't be scared. You are just a little boy. What happened is not your fault."

Amis rose angrily.

"Those are our slain warriors." Caitlin smiled. "And my father leads them. You stole our land. And his wife."

"But thou shalt not be afraid." She stood and opened her chest. "That's why I'm giving you my present today, already." She held out a red ribbon with a cameo made of a dark stone hanging from it.

Amis reached out his hand. "What's that?"

"A protection more powerful than the Cross of the Christians." Caitlin placed the amulet in his hand.

"Another superstition." Smiling, he shook his head, but his voice trembled with fright. "But it's pretty. – I'll wear it, because it's a gift from you."

The weather rarely improved in the next few days. Amis were sneaking around fearfully. One day, Caitlin showed him a snowfield in front of the castle, devastated by tracks, and the boy began to shake uncontrollably, struggling for breath. Hastily, he reached for Caitlin's amulet around his neck.

"What do you have there?" Sir Geoffrey flew in his face.

Amis' gaze went to Caitlin for help. "This..." He cleared his throat nervously. "It's just a gift from Caitlin." His eyes begged her to keep her mouth shut.

But Caitlin beamed upon Sir Geoffrey as if everything were in perfect order. "Your son has understood what counts in our land, My Lord."

"What counts?" Sir Geoffrey raised the his crop and slapped Caitlin across the chest, "I'll teach you what counts!"

The pain brought tears to her eyes, but she pressed her lips together and raised her head proudly. The triumph of having Sir Geoffrey immediately afterwards tear the amulet from Amis's neck was worth all the pain.

Another time, Caitlin and Amis found hoof marks on the beach, which were then lost on the rocky ground below a cave in the cliffs. Caitlin gave Amis a meaningful nod and observed under lowered eyelids how he paled when she suggested exploring the cave. When she wanted to go alone after his refusal, he clung to her in horror pleading not to leave him behind. With interest she observed that he was breathing hectically and barely seemed to get air. Didn't they say one could die of fear?

The evening before Epiphany added a spring tide to the blizzard, which threatened the stables in the cove where Treganna's breeding horses spent the winter. Sir Geoffrey told Amis to help the grooms rescue the horses; Caitlin volunteered. To protect the animals from the severe weather, they were taken to the higher lying caves in the cliffs.

Later, at dusk, Caitlin led Amis away from the others, to where she supposedly knew of another cave. The path trailed along the ridge of the cliff for a while. When they left the lee, something huge swept towards them in the whistling storm, beyond recognition in the heavy snowstorm. With a scream, Amis let go of his horse and ran away. On the slope down to the sea, he stumbled and then tumbled several times before he could hold on to a ledge.

Caitlin then knelt next to him and helped him sit upright.

Amis gasped in fits and starts. "What... what was that?"

"What just came at us?" Those were bushes that the wind had torn off; for Caitlin a familiar sight. But she made a worried face. "Didn't I tell you that our murdered warriors would take revenge? Today – this is their night or they must wait another year."

Amis's eyes widened in horror.

There was a noise above them; then stones pounded down next to them and rolled further downward.

"Someone's up there," stammered Amis with sallow lips. In his fear, he seemed to have forgotten that they had left their horses behind on the ridge.

Caitlin nodded, "I hear hoofbeats. Riders."

Amis wheezed and grabbed his chest. His gaze shattered.

"Treganna is mine!" Caitlin looked contemptuously at the dead child.

***

Historical notes:

The Battle of Hastings 1066, which is considered the date of the Norman conquest of England, was actually a battle for succession between a Norman descendant from the family of the Anglo-Saxon Aethelred and a Norwegian grandson of the Danish King Cnut the Great; both of them ruled England and had the same wife, one after the other.

The victorious Norman Guillaume le Conquérant (William I) imposed imposed the Norman culture and fief system on England, and a small Norman upper stratum almost completely replaced the autochthonous nobility: The Anglo-Saxons thus had well-founded reasons for their hatred.

England was Christianized in the ninth century. But for many decades the old faith lived on alongside Christianity, and were especially powerful in the regions of Celtic influence.

Pious Gifts

Ebersbach, Swabia 1754

Hildegard spied through a hole in the carriage's covering: Forest, nothing but forest. Still. A landscape in black and white. The branches bent heavily under their load. The crusted snow crunched under the wheels, while the nag was seeking its way along the barely visible path. Again and again it snorted nervously and it seemed as if it wanted to stop.

Hildegard, with teeth chattering, crawled next to her sister Margarethe under a worn horse rug.

"Hey, you are going to get your hair all messed up!" Margarethe hit her on the head with her flute. "I don't have time to fix your hair again when we arrive in Ebersbach."

Hildegard pushed herself up against the wall of the cart. "It's too late for today to play at the market. If we even arrive today, that is. Don't you see that the bay is floundering?"

"Girls, don't go and start fighting again!" Christian, their big brother on the coach box, waved the horsewhip back and forth impatiently.

Hildegard pushed aside Jacob, the youngest of the siblings, and plopped down next to Christian. She snuggled up to him. "Will you buy me new bells?"

Christian took the reins in one hand and stroked her dark curls with the other. "Do you want to dance, beautiful, or do you want to eat?"

"Tomorrow is Christmas!" Hildegard pouted. "Each of us should get a present. And the better I dance, the faster I gather the money for a marriage license."

"But first it's my turn," Margaret butted in. " I know a man who'd make me honest. I can work hard, which counts more than your pretty face."

Hildegard turned to her, twisting her lips to a sneer. "Someone with an honest trade isn't going to marry a traveler."

"I heard that in Baden they did away with the distinction," Christian made known. "There, not only shepherds and potters, but also knackers and court attendants are said to be honest people now."

"And the Walhaz and the Yeniche?" Margaret wanted to know.

"If you have money!" He shrugged. "They've always been able to buy citizenship."

Hildegard shook her head in amazement. Since when did Margaret show interest in anything other than her flutes and smart men? "Do you want to end up crawling behind city walls, Gretl? Don't make me laugh."

"You shouldn't fight all the time!" With his elbow Christian gave Hildegard a violent push into the side.

In front of the next ascent he then brought the cart to a halt. "Better get out and walk up the Raichberg."

Margaret grumbled, but Hildegard was glad to walk for a while and jumped off the cart. With one hand she lifted her skirts and with the other she grabbed the bay by its harness. In the cold air, her breath merged with that of the horse's to a cloud of mist, as she trudged through the high snow with wide strides.

Raichberg was hardly more than a hill and she soon reached the crest.

Downhill the white surface of the deforested slope glittered in the setting sun, untouched but for the traces left by small game. The view was clear all the way down to the river Fils, on which mighty chunks of ice were drifting. Behind it, the snow-covered spire of Veit Church rose between the gables of the houses.

Hildegard raised her arm in front of her face to shield her eyes from the evening sun, and followed the hustle and bustle at the bridge. The Town Guard just marched up at the bridge and closed the tollgate on the other side, behind the farmers and merchants who were leaving town.

Even those who simply wanted to go to the market outside the town would need a permit now. She sighed. So the opportunity was gone to earn a few Kreutzers and buy Christmas presents for her siblings. The next market was days away. Christian so desperately needed a new doublet and Margaret a shoulder scarf that would cover the worn elbows on her dress. And Jakob – he was growing much too quickly. Hildegard sighed again and turned to the cart.

"You were right," Margaret decreed when she had finally climbed to the crest of the hill as well. "We're too late. Another night where there's only root soup."

Hildegard shrugged, took Jakob by the hand and trudged down the snowfield with him, towards the homeward bound farmers.

"Cry," she ordered him as he stumbled down the hill next to her.

"I can't! And don't walk so fast," he whined.

"There!" She shoved him into the snow and since he still wasn't crying, she slapped him in the face without further ado.

"Hilde!" he howled.

When they arrived at the road, Jacob's face was covered with snot and tears and he was sobbing. Hildegard removed the warm red cloth covering her neck and cleavage and wrapped it around her waist.

She scrutinized the carts and appraised the horses that pulled them. Finally, she placed herself squarely in the way of the fifth one on which a middle-aged peasant sat, her arm lovingly wrapped around the crying Jacob.

"Sir, my brother is starving," she uttered in a soft voice. She sunk into a deep curtsy to afford the man a generous glimpse of her naked cleavage. "Might He have a piece of bread for him?"

The peasant licked his lips as he eyed her, and then scratched his head. "No," he said in the end.

Hildegard, looking at him steadfastly, made tears shimmer in her eyes.

"Don't cry, pretty child." He pulled his pouch out of his doublet and began to rummage through it. Hildegard saw it flash between his fingers and cast her brother a furtive glance. Jacob cried louder and drew nearer. The peasant looked up and handed the boy a half Kreutzer. "Here, with this you can eat your fill tomorrow."

"The Lord bless you." Hildegard curtsied once again and approached him close enough that her hip touched his leg. "I thank the good Sir that He has bestowed a Christmas upon us." Her eyes flashed and a smile deepened the dimples in her face.

The peasant reached out and stroked her cheek, reddened by the frost, with rough fingers. Then he turned to the back of his cart and opened one of the crates piled up. He took out two eggs and a hard sausage and gave them to Hildegard. "So you don't go to sleep hungry." He smiled at her and urged his horse on.

Jacob tugged at her skirts.

"Quiet!" She pulled him off the road. After a few steps uphill, she turned around once more and looked back at the peasant. "Run!"

In front of the cart on the Raichberg a fire was already burning; Margarethe was filling the cauldron with snow.

While the bells of Veit Church sounded to them, Hildegard placed the two eggs and the sausage in her lap.

"At least something." Margarethe nodded approvingly.

"We have even more!" Jakob, with eyes gleaming, pulled the half Kreutzer from his pocket.

Hildegard moistened her red cloth with the snow. "We'd better not come with you when you go into town tomorrow." Gently, she wiped the dirt off Jakob's face.

Christian smirked. "I thought you wanted to look for a sweetheart?"

"I'll find one when I need one." Hildegard repeated Jakob's words: "We have even more!"

She reached into her skirt pocket and took out the peasant's pouch. "Blessed Christmas."

***

Historical note:

The city ordinances in the early modern period and the guild system were characterized by a well-developed social system. But poor relief aimed only to protect and provide for their own citizens and their widows and orphans. The guild system, moreover, was designed on the one hand to guarantee the quality of craftsmanship, but on the other to keep competitors away.

Those who had something to offer could, of course,

settle in a town. Or marry in. "Vagrants" – and these were not only the gypsies, but also a part of the so-called dishonest trades – didn't however have a chance at citizens' rights. They couldn't even buy an apprenticeship for their children, which would have gained them access to one of the guilds. In addition to minstrels, tinkers, and similar trades of the vagrants also gravediggers, knackers, and even shepherds, millers, and barbers were among the dishonest trades.

In many towns, vagrants were not even tolerated as beggars, so they almost inevitably had to become criminals in order to survive.

Bread

Paris, 16 Floréal III (May 5, 1795)

Change of guards at the gendarmerie on *Rue de la Tixeran-derie*: Jean-Pierre Chalandon greeted his replacement with a gloomy gaze. "Tonight we fished four pregnant women out of the Seine. We could save only one of them; Claire, the daughter of the old seamstress Dechamps."

"I know," answered Michel. "I saw you take her home."

"You were still awake that late? It was almost four."

"I was up that early," replied Michel. "And I also know that Claire has meanwhile given birth. The little girl weighs not even four pounds. The midwife has little hope that she will survive for long."

"This misery is a crime," said Jean-Pierre. "And it's getting even worse every day: As of today, everyone in our quarter is allotted only two ounces of bread."

"Yet the citizens who can afford to pay ten *livres* and more for a pound of white bread indulge in *brioches* and *croissants*," hissed Michel. "But then I have to stand again in front of Robillard's bakery to prevent the angry women from kicking in his door."

"Yet he really deserves a beating. Last week he was reported once more for processing low-grade flour. It cries out to Heaven how this pack grows rich on the poor people; but God has been abolished."

"And reporting doesn't help at all."

Jean-Pierre reached for his jacket and left the station. It was still dark, but the women were already queuing up everywhere.I n front of many shops they would wait in vain. Today again, there were no vegetables and no butter. The quarter's Committee of Public Safety had informed him that once again no supplier had made it past the Faubourg Saint-Antoine into the city. The female citizens in the suburbs had plundered them all.

He jingled the *sous* in his jacket pocket and smiled despite everything as he walked down the street under the blossoming chestnuts. It was a May day, the likes that couldn't be more beautiful in Paris, and it was his wife's birthday.

He wanted to surprise her with a good piece of meat. He knew a butcher at St. Catherine's market who still owed him a favor, because he had caught him selling rationed meat to a paper manufacturer's cook. Certainly he would still have to pay far more than the General Maximum allowed by law, but today he didn't care.

In front of Robillard's bakery on Rue de la Jussienne Jean-Pierre came upon an agitated crowd. The door to the shop was wide open, but no trace of Robillard. "*Citoyennes*, what's going on here?"

Widow Leclerc's answer was barely audible in the babble of voices. "...is in the bakery," reached Jean-Pierre's ear.

"He is hanging in the bakery," called out Nanette, her neighbor.

Jean-Pierre rushed inside. The baker was hanging from a beam above a large trough with a flour sack over his head. The dough, which had risen too high in the meantime, was surging from the trough.

This was murder. Horrified, Jean-Pierre stared at the scene in front of him and stopped to avoid destroying any traces. The murder of a baker was the last thing he needed. Undecided what to do now, he looked around. His shift was actually over, and if he didn't go to the market immediately, he wouldn't get any meat at all.

Twenty unbaked *flutes* were lying on the wooden slider next to the oven; on the table next to them, countless raw *brioches*. The fire was glowing only weakly now. Jean-Pierre opened the door of the oven: charred *baguettes*.

A noise made him turn around with a start: From under the flour sacks, a rat scurried out. Forgetting all caution, he stepped closer and opened one of the sacks. Inside it was swarming with maggots. "Boo!" Disgust shook him.

The question of what now resolved itself, when Inspector Roux arrived at the scene. "Good morning, citizen Chalandon. Have you discovered anything yet?"

"Well, the murder must have happened between three and four o'clock. Robillard already had the first bread in the oven, but no opportunity to get out the finished *baguettes*. And the murderer was too early for that, too."

"Or he wasn't interested in the bread."

"Do you really believe that anyone would leave even a bit of bread behind?"

"No," the inspector admitted. "I actually can't imagine that. But maybe he's been interrupted."

Jean-Pierre shook his head. "at that hour, usually no one is out on the street. And if there had been, then I would have seen him too. It was shortly after half past three, when I brought Claire home. I passed by here; and once again on my way back to the gendarmerie."

Roux twirled his mustache; "Too bad! I guess you just missed the murderer."

"If anyone had been on the street, I surely would have..." His voice faltered. Michel! Michel must have been on the street. Why hadn't he seen him? And why hadn't Michel talked to him?

"What is it? Did you indeed notice anything?"

After a brief hesitation, Jean-Pierre shook his head. "No, inspector. I can't help you any further. – And now I must hurry to the market. Today is Charlotte's birthday."

"Well, run along then. Congratulate her from me and have a nice day you two."

Yet despite all the haste, Jean-Pierre did not go directly to the market, but back to the station. He wanted to talk with Michel. At the gendarmerie, however, he learned that the meeting place of the Committee of Public Safety was besieged by rebellious housewives and Michel, together with some colleagues, had been ordered to protect the members of the committee.

His visit to the market, on the other hand, was a complete success. Jean-Pierre not only got a big piece of lamb shoulder for his savings, but could also purchase a good bottle of red wine and even two eggs. This would not only make dinner a celebration, but also secure the next breakfast. After dropping off his treasures at home, he did not want to sit idly by until Charlotte got home. He had to talk to Michel.

Not only the housewives of the quarter had gathered in front of the Committee of Public Safety, but also some male citizens. "Bread and the constitution of 1793," Jean-Pierre heard them shout from afar. The crowd stood densely packed on the square in front of the driveway to the building; Michel and the other gendarmes were facing them, their pistols drawn.

"The commissaries stole the flour that was for our children," the women yelled at the policemen. Furiously, they waved pans and rolling pins. "In the name of the sovereign people and the law: It's your duty to arrest them."

"We did not swindle you," a voice came from the first

floor. A member of the committee had ventured to the open window: "You have elected us. You do have no right to give orders. This is revolt!"

"Yes, this is revolt," countered a young girl in the first row, the ironer Josephine Rouillière. "You are disposed. We'll immediately vote in others." She turned around; her gaze went over the crowd, searching for the few men present. "Citizen Moreau! – Citizen Duplessis! – Citizen Grimond! – Citizen Fielval!" –

Jean-Pierre wished to become invisible when her gaze went in his direction. – "Citizen Chalandon, wonderful!" She beamed at him. "I propose voting you in as members of the Committee of Public Safety."

In light of the shouts of affirmation, Moreau pushed to the front and took the stand. "*Citoyennes*, we thank you for your trust." He nodded at Jean-Pierre and the three other newly elected commissaries. Then he turned to the gendarmes. "You've heard. Put away your pistols and come with us! The committee is to be arrested."

After a glance at Jean-Pierre, Michel put away his weapon; the others followed his example. They acknowledged the vote: the confrontation between the people and the gendarmes was over.

At this moment, a unit of soldiers turned into the street led by four delegates to the National Convention.

Upon sight of them, a cry of "Help!" came from the first floor.

"Stop!" Jean-Pierre shouted to the soldiers. "We don't need your help. It's all settled."

But the next moment, there was a bang behind him. A shot had come from the first floor!

Shouting irately, the women pushed open the gate to the driveway; nothing could stop them now. As the gendarmes moved aside, Jean-Pierre saw that one of them was supporting Michel. He rushed towards them.

Below Michel's left shoulder, a blood stain spread quickly. Groaning, he leaned against the wall of the building and pressed his right hand at the wound. "Citizen Chalandon!" A touch of mockery laced his voice. "What are you doing here? Aren't you supposed to be celebrating with Charlotte?"

"I have a question for you." Jean-Pierre chewed on his lower lip for a moment. Then he went close to Michel and whispered, "You, what were you doing so early this morning on Rue de la Jussienne? – You saw us passing Robillard's place, didn't you?"

Michel's pale face turned an even whiter shade of pale. Then he nodded. "So, I talked too much this morning, again. But now it doesn't matter anymore."

"It doesn't matter," confirmed Jean-Pierre softly as Michel passed out. "No one else other than I heard it."

Two days later Michel died in the hospital.

***

Historical notes:

In revolutionary France, from 1792, the Christian calendar was no longer in use. The decimal system, introduced in 1790, was also applied to the Republican calendar. The year had twelve months of thirty days, the week ten numbered days. In order to align with the "tropical year," five to six additional days were inserted at the end of each year.

The names of the months referred either to the French climate or peasant activities, the days were named after plants, animals, and tools rather than the Christian saints.

The Republican calendar was in use until 1806, as well as for two weeks during the Commune of Paris 1871. *It took effect on the 15th of* Vendémiaire *(harvest month) of year II (6 October 1793), even before all terms had been finalized. The calendar itself, however, began with the 1st* Vendémiaire *of year I (September 22, 1792), the day of the proclamation of the Republic, as the first day of the new era.*

1 onze *(ounce) corresponded with 30 grams. Bread was the staple food of the common people. That's why riots were ignited by increases in bread prices.*

Livre: *a unit of account that existed in two different ranges: the* Livre tournois *and the* Livre parisis. *The coins of the Ancien Régime (the two centuries before the Revolution) were based on the* Livre tournois. *The* Livre *itself, though, never existed as a coin until the French Revolution. In August 1795 it was replaced by the* Franc.

The Wheels of Justice

Lucerne, 1824

Michael Corragioni, Lucerne's city doctor, banged a slender file onto the sheriff's bureau. "Here's your body, Mr. Am Rhyn. Strangled. The man was already dead when he fell into the Reuss."

"So, do we have it accurate this time?" Karl Am Rhyn did not look up, but continued to whittle on his quill with concentration. This report could wait; the dead vagrant was in no hurry anymore.

"What are you getting at?" Corragioni raised his eyebrows.

"At that time, you weren't able of making any statements about sheriff Keller." From the corner of his eye, Am Rhyn observed Corragioni as he went on. "And right now rumors are getting strengthened that my predecessor didn't accidentally drown in the Reuss."

Corragioni shrugged. "Those rumors surface with every dead body we fish out." He seemed to be waiting for a retort, but Am Rhyn put away his quill and began leafing through the file. He had no intention of explaining his remark in more detail.

"*Papist!*" he mumbled when the city doctor had left. Then he called for his son, who served as his assistant. "Toni, has the magistrate of Glarus meanwhile sent any further information about this thief?"

"He won't send any further information, but he sends the wench herself for interrogation, and also her brother. It's all very dubious: The accounts this person gave about the circumstances of the crime don't match what we told the magistrate."

As soon as Clara Wendel arrived at the prison in Lucerne, the sheriff had her brought for questioning. He waited for her in an unheated room in the basement of the courthouse.

The gendarme brought a young woman in a traditional, short-sleeved dress to him. Her brown eyes had kept their shine despite the long detention. And her black hair was carefully braided to a long plait. Only a split lip and a bluish-yellow bruise under her right eye detracted from her even face.

"She has lied," Am Rhyn bellowed bluntly at her. "Not even the biggest idiot fishes at night in the rain."

Clara lowered her gaze. "I have truly told you what I have heard myself about that incident."

"She claimed She were there at the time."

"But I don't really remember anything. How distinguishes a child between what she experiences herself and what is told to her."

"So She also cannot distinguish whether it is true or a lie," remarked the sheriff. He rose and walked around his bureau. Right in front of her he stopped.

Clara avoided his gaze and pressed her hands together.

"Well?"

"If it weren't true, would I have named my own brother ?"

"Then She tell me again what really happened."

"I've already said everything, I can't think of anything else."

"Then we will give Her memory some help." The sheriff waved over the guard who approached with his club raised.

Clara screamed and raised her arms in front of her face. "Don't hit me; I'll tell Him what I know."

Am Rhyn turned to the side, reached for his pipe, filled it slowly and lit it. The guard ran the club twice down Clara's back. She whimpered and fell to her knees.

"She opens her mouth, then She'll be left alone," said the sheriff, without looking her way.

"I'm freezing," she whispered. She crouched on the stone floor and wrapped her arms around her knees.

"Which of Her statements are lies?" asked Am Rhyn. "No question about it, She lied."

The guard raised his club once again; Clara peered at him from the corner of her eye and began to quiver. "I think, there was a tailor, a certain Joseph or Aloys Meyer, who held a grudge against the sheriff. Hansi was already in the area for several days and had spied it out. I suppose, he knew what he was waiting for. On the day in question, I went with my mother to Littauen, where we set something on fire. After that we went back; Hansi was waiting for us and we continued. And then it just happened, as I said it did."

Am Rhyn put his pipe aside to observe her reactions. "Why is She bringing a tailor into it now?" That was a twist he liked very much. It could lead to entirely new insights.

"I suppose, Hansi had an instigator. What could my brother have had with the sheriff?

"What could the tailor have had with the sheriff?"

Clara shrugged and smiled in Am Rhyn's face. "I'm just saying."

"So She made that up!" He moved so close to her his frock coat hit her in the face. "Who is She covering for?"

"I've told everything I know." She lowered her head. He barely understood her mumbling. "I just thought so. He must have had a reason, the tailor."

"Exactly!" Am Rhyn leaned down to her familiarly. "Might he, too, have had an instigator? Did you ever hear of anything to let you think that?"

"I don't know. I must first bethink myself a bit more on the matter."

"So bethink it." The sheriff left her alone with the guard.

Am Rhyn's daughter-in-law had invited him to dinner in the evening. He hardly noticed what he was eating, and simply waited to retreat to the library with his son.

"The wench says whatever comes to her mind, but in between it all, she does betray quite a bit."

Toni gave him an expectant look as he took the cognac and two bulbous snifters from the glass cabinet.

Am Rhyn took a glass and let him pour a drink. He sniffed the cognac and smiled. "I am sure we are on the track of a conspiracy. Finally, we'll find out how Keller was killed."

"He drowned! We've never found any evidence that the rumors might be true."

"And yet it was murder!" Am Rhyn placed his glass so violently on the table that the cognac spilled over. "Keller was on Napoleon's side right from the beginning and persistently fought against replacing the Act of Mediation with a conservative constitution. He was our bulwark against the Ultramontanes." With fierce gestures, Am Rhyn filled his pipe. "You have not seen how Corragioni and the papal nuncio were seething, when he damned the restoration by the Congress of Vienna."

"But that is still a long way from needing Keller dead. Just look how far away we are today from a federal state."

"Why did the Pope recall the nuncio to the Roman curia so suddenly? After all, he supported Testaferrata's conservative church policy."

"When Testaferrata was recalled, Keller was still alive."

"So what? The clerics have long arms." Am Rhyn shook his head. "You are certainly naïve." Couldn't his son put two and two together?

"No, Father. I think you are getting stuck in something that will only bring you harm in the end. What do you want with the statements of a thief who was still a child at the time of Keller's death? If you are wrong, then the Ultramontanes will be afloat more than ever."

"I'm not mistaken." Am Rhyn rose. "We don't need to talk any more. You'll see."

Clara was pale when brought again the next morning. Her blood-encrusted hood only half covered a fresh laceration at her hairline.

"What does She have to report meanwhile about Keller's death? Just speak freely and spare none."

"Should I recite the course of events once again?"

"But no, the one detail or the other is not important." Am Rhyn stood and pushed Clara to the window. He put his arm around her and pointed to the patrician house at the Reuss bridge, next to which the two onion towers of the Jesuit church were reflected in the water. "Do you know who lives there? Have you ever heard of anyone who had anything to do with the occupants?"

She looked from the building to the church and back again. Then she shook her head. "Those are fine people. I don't know people like that."

"Eight years ago, someone broke in over there."

"I was most definitely not there. But I wouldn't put my hand in the fire for my people. Perhaps something might come to me when the Sir Sheriff tell me what was stolen."

"Have you perhaps ever heard of someone being discovered in a burglary, but wasn't reported?" He observed her from the corners of his eyes.

"Yes, of course... But that always comes with a price."

"Did that happen to your brother, too?"

"Not to Hansi, but to Sepp, my brother-in-law."

"What do you know about it?"

"He's a good lad, Sepp."

Am Rhyn lowered the corners of his mouth.

"Yes, really," Clara quickly asserted. "He resigned from the military, where he had a proper wage, because he wanted to be a father to his children. And he's smart; he's seen half the world." She gazed at the river, pulled on her braid. Then she looked at Am Rhyn, her eyes alert: "I suppose, when someone breaks in somewhere and the master of the house discovers him and lets him go, then it wasn't really a crime, was it?"

"Unless a person is accused, he cannot be judged. So talk."

"I can't tell you anything more about it. I only know of it from Barbara. He came back entirely harried, so said the sister." Clara leaned her head against the window and closed her eyes. "I am hungry."

"She'll be used to. She tell me what She heard."

She sank to the floor. "I feel entirely miserable."

The sheriff failed to be impressed. "When anything else comes back to Her, then we'll talk further." He turned to the door. "Enjoy your meal!" he greeted the guard on his way out.

Am Rhyn rushed into his son's office. "The wench recognized the house!" He beamed at Toni. "Her brother-in-law was surprised by Corragioni. But he let him go. I still remember the incident exactly: The city doctor reported a break-in shortly before Keller's death, but couldn't give any details of what had been stolen."

Toni put his quill back into the inkwell, folded his hands and rested his head on them. He studied his father and didn't say a word.

Am Rhyn fell into an armchair. "The noose is tightening. Papists, vile."

"Did Wendel testify to that?"

"She admitted that Twerenhold has once just barely got away. But she's afraid he could still be charged for it today. So she was hemming and hawing."

Toni stood from the bureau and sat in the armchair opposite him. "Father, You're getting carried away! Twerenhold only came back from the Netherlands in 1820."

"Then he made good use of a leave, and not only for copulating." Am Rhyn guffaed at his joke. "In any case, after the break-in, the city doctor had him in his grip; that's obvious."

Toni sighed. "You have no proof; no proof of anything. Not even a proper statement from this person. And with her bad reputation, she's no valid witness, especially not on her own."

"We'll find the witnesses as soon as she has told us everything she knows. We already have her brother; we'll get the brother-in-law. And I'll subpoena the tailor, too. He is entirely respectable. So his statement carries weight."

"Didn't she report the tailor as instigator?"

"You can't believe that person that much," grumbled Am Rhyn. He was irritated by Toni's endless objections. "I've always thought Corragioni was behind it; now I can finally prove it. He won't get away from me anymore!"

The sheriff began the next interrogation with a beating. When

Clara was reduced to whimpering, he grabbed her by the braid and pulled her to the window again. "My patience is slowly coming to an end. Admit what She knows about the break-in over there."

"I wasn't there."

"Two days ago She testified that She were out thieving in the area with Her mother. And the brother was already waiting. Where were the brother-in-law and sister in that time?"

"Sepp was not there!"

"Did he ever mention the name Corragioni? Does She know, who that is?"

"Yes, he's the city doctor. The gendarmes summoned Barbara back then."

"Then She does know, who lives over there!"

"I wasn't there!"

"So She wants to deny everything again? She hasn't had enough?"

The guard understood the question as an instruction and struck again. Clara was thrown against the wall from the impact of the blow; she cried out and put her hands to her face.

"Well then? Who did Sepp talk to about the city doctor?"

"He once said to Hansi that he were a gentleman. Not like the others who merely pay lip service to the mercifulness of God."

"What was that supposed to mean?"

"I don't know." The next blow made her laceration bleed again. "I suppose, he was grateful to him."

"And for that, the brother-in-law would be obliging? And he immediately roped in Her brother? That's what She means, isn't it?"

Clara made a movement with her head, which Am Rhyn interpreted as a nod.

"And then Hansi pushed Keller into the Reuss. That was, after all, Her brother who was incited to do it. That's what She testified, didn't She?" He pulled her up and pushed her against the window.

Clara remained silent.

"Did She or did She not name Her brother?"

"Yes, sure, but..."

"...but it was Twerenhold? Did She simply name Her brother because he was going to hang anyway?"

"No! The brother-in-law didn't kill anyone."

The sheriff left her and went to see the magistrate. "Have Corragioni arrested. Immediately. Wendel confessed that he blackmailed her brother-in-law to murder Keller." Exhausted from running, Am Rhyn fell into an armchair.

"The testimony of a thief doesn't count. Karl, I can't have a respected member of the Diet arrested on that." The magistrate shook his head at the sheriff's zeal.

"We also need the confession of the perpetrator; I know that well enough. We'll get to it. We have the brother, don't we?"

"Then come back when you have the confession."

Am Rhyn jumped; his face turned red. "But when he realizes we're on to him, Corragioni will hightail it, like the nuncio did back then."

"What are you bringing in the nuncio now?"

"When the new Pope authorized the Jesuits again, Testafarrata wanted to bring them back to Lucerne. Keller prevented it back then."

"And that's how it stayed. So no one had an advantage from his death"

"No one knew that beforehand. Don't be so stubborn!" shouted Am Rhyn. "Get Corragioni arrested before it's too late."

The magistrate looked at him imperturbably. "Bring me the murderer's confession. Then you can have him."

***

Historical Note:

After the German Campaign of 1813, Europe was reorganized at the Congress of Vienna in 1814/1815. For Switzerland, this resulted in a decades-long struggle over its political constitutionality. The conservative forces wanted to return to the conditions before the revolution of 1798, while the liberals were took their ideas from Napoleon's Act of Mediation, who had abolished the national parliament and the central government and shifted most of the power to the Cantons. The readmission of the Jesuits also played a role in this situation, since it was significant for the school system.

Against this background rumors persisted that the liberal-democratic sheriff Keller had been murdered: He drowned in the Reuss in 1816. The statements of his daughters, as well as all the other circumstances, however, spoke for an accident; eight years later, though, the rumors re-ignited with the statements of a young vagrant.

The Catholic medical counselor Michael Leodegar Corragioni d'Orelli, member of the Grand Council and the Small Council of the Canton of Lucerne, was charged in 1826 with instigation of the murder of sheriff Franz Xaver Keller and put on trial together with Clara Wendel's clan of vagrants.

He was acquitted. The confessions of the vagrants, which had been extorted under torture, for once held less weight than political considerations.

Clara Wendel also survived the trial, whereas others from her clan were executed.

***

Thank your for reading.
If you liked these stories, please consider leaving a review at your favorite bookstore. Recommendations and reviews help others to find books worth reading.

About the author

Annemarie Nikolaus began literary writing at the beginning of 2001. She now publishes her work independently.
She was born in Hessia/Germany and lived in Northern Italy for 20 years. In 2010, she moved to the Auvergne in France with her daughter.

After studying psychology, journalism, politics and history, she worked as a psychotherapist, political consultant, and journalist, among others.

Blog in English: http://bit.ly/2G0ugGJ

Subscribe to her Newsletter, if you want to know about new books: http://eepurl.com/bHQtvf

You can find Annemarie on:
Patreon: www.patreon.com/AnnemarieNikolaus
Facebook: http://ow.ly/bVOE5
Twitter : http://twitter.com/AnneNikolaus

****

Publications:

In English:

Magical Stories. Short stories for children. Paperback edition ISBN 9782902412600.

Radiant Hope. Illustrated science-fiction story. Paperback edition ISBN 9782902412600.

The Granddaughter. *"Quick, quick, slow - Lietzensee Dance Club".* Paperback edition ISBN 9782493398123

Back onto the Dance Floor. *"Quick, quick, slow - Lietzensee Dance Club".* Paperback edition ISBN 9782493398147.

Falling for a movie star. *"Quick, quick, slow - Lietzensee Dance Club".* Paperback edition ISBN 9782493398130

Broken Rules. Historical crime short stories. Paperback edition ISBN 9782902412686

Silenced. Short thriller. Paperback edition ISBN 978-xx

Gone... Short Stories. Paperback edition ISBN 9782902412877.

The Piratess. *"Dragon World"* series. Fantasy novel. Paperback edition ISBN 9782902412679

Aquitaine: The End of a War. *"By The Wayside..."* series. Paperback edition ISBN 9782902412808

In German:

Novels and short stories

Historical

Königliche Republik. *"Welt in Flammen"* series. Historical novel. Paperback edition ISBN 9782902412471

Verjährt. Historical crime short stories. Paperback edition ISBN 9782902412549.

Fantasy

Die Piratin. *"Drachenwelt"* series. Fantasy novel. Paperback edition ISBN 9782902412495

Das Feuerpferd. Fantasy novel, together with Monique Lhoir und Sabine Abel. Paperback edition ISBN 9782902412501

Magische Geschichten. Short stories for children and adults. Paperback edition ISBN 9782902412488

Renntag in Kruschar. *"Drachenwelt"* series. Fantasy anthology. E-Book only

Leuchtende Hoffnung. A Science Fiction novel in Advent calendar form. Paperback edition ISBN 9782902412563

Crime

Bitterer Wein. »Médoc« series. Mystery. Paperback edition ISBN 782493398017

Haus zu verkaufen. Family drama. Paperback edition ISBN 9782902412983

Ustica. Short story thriller. Paperback edition ISBN 9782902412556. Paperback with voucher for the e-Book.

Tot. Short stories. Paperback edition ISBN 9782902412587.

Verjährt. (see above)

Romance

Die Enkelin. *'Quick, quick, slow - Tanzclub Lietzensee'* series. Love story. Paperback edition ISBN 9782493398093.

Flirt mit einem Star. *'Quick, quick, slow - Tanzclub Lietzensee'* series. Love story. Paperback edition ISBN 9782493398109

Zurück aufs Parkett. *'Quick, quick, slow - Tanzclub Lietzensee'* series. Story of love and marriage. Paperback edition ISBN 9782493398116

Non-fiction

Tourist attractions

Aquitanien: Das Ende eines Krieges. *"Am Rande des Weges ..."* series. Paperback edition ISBN 9782902412570

Background series on literature and books

Suche Reisebegleitung. *Fliegende Blätter.* Paperback edition ISBN 9781499608427

Junge Welten. *Fliegende Blätter.* Paperback edition ISBN 9781500971991